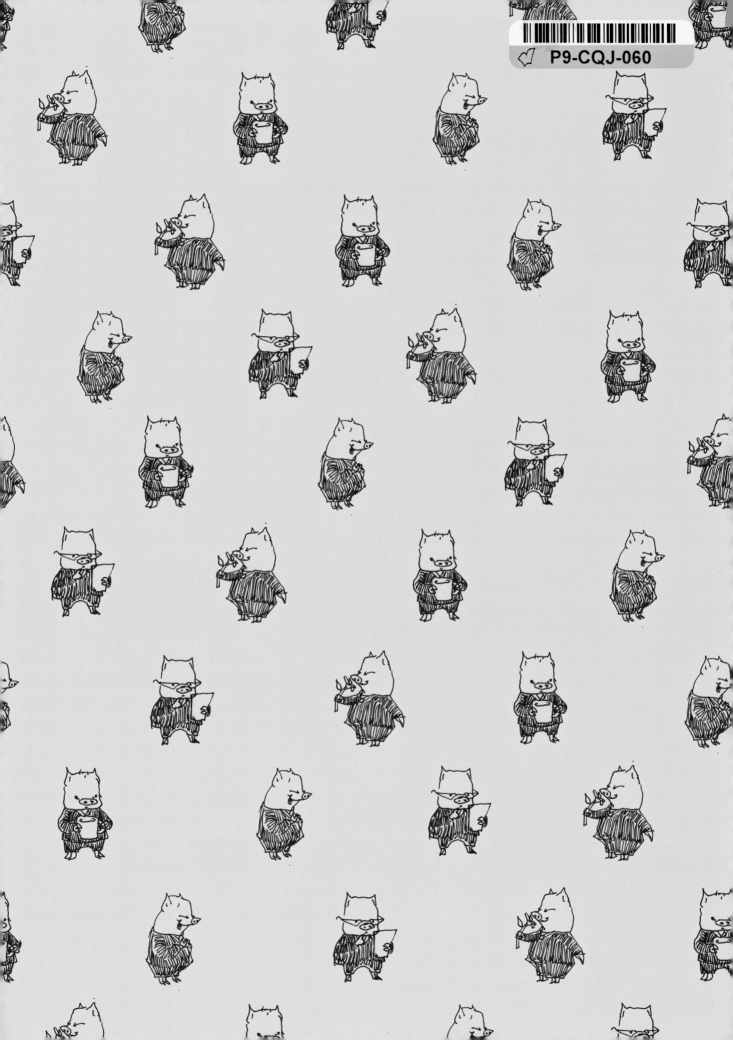

For Amy.
Because she and she alone
knows the reason I created this book.
—A. Z.

STERLING CHILDREN'S BOOKS
New York

An Imprint of Sterling Publishing Co., Inc.
1166 Avenue of the Americas
New York, NY 10036

ISBN 978-1-4549-2684-9

Distributed in Canada by Sterling Publishing Co., Inc.
c/o Canadian Manda Group, 664 Annette Street
Toronto, Ontario M6S 2C8, Canada
Distributed in the United Kingdom by GMC Distribution Services
Castle Place, 166 High Street, Lewes, East Sussex BN7 1XU, England
Distributed in Australia by NewSouth Books
45 Beach Street, Coogee, NSW 2034, Australia

For information about custom editions, special sales, and premium and corporate
purchases, please contact Sterling Special Sales at 800-805-5489
or specialsales@sterlingpublishing.com.

Manufactured in China

Lot #:
2 4 6 8 10 9 7 5 3 1
06/18

sterlingpublishing.com

Cover and interior design by Irene Vandervoort

Business
Pig

Words and Pictures by
ANDREA ZUILL

STERLING CHILDREN'S BOOKS
New York

One morning at the Sunshine Sanctuary for Farm Animals, Jelly Bean the sow gave birth to a litter of piglets. Right away the volunteers noticed something unusual.

Jasper was very different from his siblings.

He hated
playing in the mud.

And he refused to
root for grubs,
acorns, and other
tasty things the way
the other pigs did.

Everyone at the sanctuary loved little Jasper.
But that didn't keep him from feeling out of place.

The volunteers decided to create a space just for him.
He liked it very much.

They also let him help with the bookkeeping.

The whole barnyard would turn out for his meetings to show their support.

Still, not everyone
appreciated what
Jasper had to offer.
The chickens
continually refused to
take an interest in
his flow charts.

And the goat ate his business card.

Worst of all, no matter how many
charts he presented

or résumés he handed out
expounding on why he would
make a great pet . . .

... he was passed up for adoption. It was quite disheartening. It really was.

Sigh...

But Jasper was a smart, outgoing, proactive pig—
and not one to let life get him down for long.
He formed a plan.

First, he approached the media.

Then he enlisted the help of some of his contacts.

He even used some old-fashioned,
tried-and-true methods to get his message out.

Satisfied with a job well done, Jasper took some time
to relax and wonder if all his efforts would pay off.

Immediately Jasper saw results.
Someone soon visited the farm, someone who
did not look like the average person planning
to adopt a forever farm pet.

He was pleased to see she was actually
studying his charts!

She wanted to exchange business cards with him.

Then she requested
his résumé,

and read it
thoroughly.

The interview went well.
But upper management had to be consulted.

Luckily, upper management was also impressed
with Jasper's credentials.
Everything added up. The offer was made and
the contract was signed.

It was a perfect fit!